This book belongs to

Jack Horne

Age 3

Puss in Boots

RETOLD BY

Samantha Easton

ILLUSTRATED BY

Debbie Dieneman

LEOPARD

This edition published in 1995 by Leopard Books,
20 Vauxhall Bridge Road, London SW1V 2SA

First published in 1992 by Andrews and McMeel

ISBN 0 7529 0110 9

Design: Susan Hood and Mike Hortens
Art Direction: Armand Eisen, Mike Hortens and Julie Phillips
Art Production: Lynn Wine
Production: Julie Miller and Lisa Shadid

Puss in Boots

$\mathcal{T}$here was once an old miller who had three sons. When the miller died, he left to his sons his mill, his donkey, and his cat. As was the custom, the eldest son inherited the mill. The second son received the donkey, and the third got only the cat.

Now, the third son was very good-natured, and he accepted his inheritance cheerfully. Nevertheless, when he was alone, he could

not help sighing, "How lucky my brothers are! With a mill and a donkey they will be able to live comfortably, but with only a cat I shall surely starve if I do not soon find work!"

To the young man's surprise, the cat, who had been listening from the corner, said, "Do not despair, my good master. I am not as useless as I look. Get me a sack and a pair of leather boots so that I may tramp around the countryside without hurting my paws. Then you shall see what I can do for you."

"A cat that can speak as well as that must be clever," thought the young man. So he took all the money he had and bought the cat a canvas sack and a fine pair of leather boots.

The cat was delighted when he saw the boots and put them on at once.

"My, how fine you look!" said the young man, laughing a little, for the cat looked so pleased with himself. "From now on I shall call you Puss in Boots!"

"You may call me whatever you like," replied the cat. "But now I am off to make your fortune."

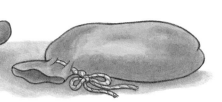

Puss in Boots filled his canvas bag with carrots. Then he stalked off to a rabbit warren that was full of plump, young rabbits.

He opened his bag, then stretched out on the ground beside it and lay very still. Presently some curious rabbits ran into the bag to eat the carrots. At once, Puss in Boots leaped up and tied the bag shut with the rabbits still inside.

Then, feeling very proud of his catch, he went to the palace and asked to see the king himself. The king's servants had never seen a cat wearing fine leather boots before. They were so amazed, they immediately led Puss in Boots to his majesty's throne room.

Puss in Boots bowed low to the king. "Greetings, your majesty," he said. "These rabbits come from my master's warren, and he has asked me to make you a present of them."

"How kind," said the king. "Pray, tell me, what is your master's name?"

"He is the Marquis of Carabas," Puss in Boots replied grandly, though the miller's son was called no such thing.

"Then kindly thank him for me," said the king. "And tell him that I am very pleased."

Puss in Boots said that he would do so and returned home.

The next day, Puss in Boots filled his canvas bag with corn. Then he went to a place in the country where many wild pheasants nested. Opening the bag wide, he stretched out beside it and lay very still. Presently, a number of pheasants ran inside to eat the corn. Then Puss in Boots quickly tied the bag shut and once again went to the king.

Puss in Boots bowed low before his

majesty and said, "My lord, the Marquis of
Carabas has asked me to give you these
pheasants as a token of his esteem."

"My, how very thoughtful!" said the king.
"I only hope someday I can repay your
master's kindness."

Puss in Boots was very glad to hear this.
When he had bid good-bye to the king, he
rushed home to the miller's son.

"Listen, master,"
Puss in Boots said that
night, "I have a plan
that will make your
fortune. Tomorrow
morning I will take you
to a place along the
river where you will go
swimming. Do as I say
and I will take care of
the rest."

The miller's son could not understand
how this would make his fortune. But he
thought, "The cat certainly seems to know
what he is doing." So he agreed to do as Puss
in Boots had asked.

Early the next morning Puss in Boots led
the miller's son to a part of the river that ran
beside the king's palace. Then the miller's
son went swimming, leaving his clothes on
the bank.

Puss in Boots hid his master's clothes under a rock. Then he shouted as loudly as he could, "Help! Help! My master, the Marquis of Carabas, is about to be drowned!"

Now, as Puss in Boots knew quite well, the king walked along that part of the river every morning. Sure enough, soon the king came walking down the road with his daughter, the princess. When he heard Puss in Boots' cries, he ordered his guards to leap into the river at once and save the Marquis of Carabas.

While the guards were pulling the miller's son to shore, Puss in Boots told the king that wicked robbers had set upon his master and stolen all his clothes.

"How terrible!" cried the king. Then he ordered his servants to fetch one of his best suits of clothes for the unfortunate Marquis to wear.

When the miller's son was dressed in royal clothes, he looked so handsome that the princess instantly fell in love with him.

Puss in Boots watched how the princess smiled at the miller's son. This was just what he had hoped would happen. He took his master aside and whispered, "Tell the king and the princess that if only your carriage hadn't been stolen, you would gladly invite them to see your palace to repay them for their kindness."

"What are you saying?" the miller's son cried. "I have no palace!"

"Do as I tell you," said Puss in Boots. "And you shall soon have the princess for a wife."

Now, the miller's son had fallen as much in love with the princess as she had with him. So he eagerly agreed, although he could not imagine what his cat intended to do.

The king was very pleased by the invitation and quickly accepted. "My daughter and I would be overjoyed to visit your palace," the king exclaimed. "We shall go there at once in my carriage!" So Puss in Boots gave the king's coachman instructions, and they prepared to set out.

   While the king and the princess and the miller's son waited for the carriage to be made ready, Puss in Boots ran ahead.

   Down the road he came upon a group of people mowing a large meadow. Puss in Boots called to them in a mournful voice, "Oh, my good people, be careful or you will surely lose your heads today!"

   "What do you mean?" asked one of them.

   "The king is coming with his guards," said Puss in Boots. "He will stop and ask you to whom this meadow belongs. You must answer the Marquis of Carabas, for if you do not the king's soldiers will chop off your heads at once!"

"Never fear," replied one of the men. "We will do so without fail!"

Soon the king came passing by. When he saw the large meadow, he ordered the carriage to stop. "Tell me, my good people," he asked, "to whom does this meadow belong?"

"Why, sir! To the Marquis of Carabas!" they all replied at once.

"Ah," said the king, looking very pleased. "A very fine meadow it is, too." And he ordered the carriage to move on.

Meanwhile Puss in Boots had run on ahead. Presently, he came to a huge field of corn where people were busy harvesting. Puss in Boots stopped and called to them in a gloomy voice. "Oh, my good people," he cried, "please be very, very careful today. Otherwise, I fear you will surely lose your heads!"

"What are you saying?" they asked.

"The king is coming with all his guards," replied Puss in Boots. "He will ask you to whom this field of corn belongs. You must answer 'To the Marquis of Carabas.' If you don't— well, you can imagine what the king's men will do then!"

"Don't worry," said one of the workers. "We will certainly give the king the answer he wants!"

So when the king came by a moment later and asked the workers to whom the great cornfield belonged, they all replied at once, "Why, to the Marquis of Carabas, your majesty!"

And on it went. Every time the king passed something and asked to whom it belonged, the answer was always the same: "This belongs to the Marquis of Carabas, your majesty!"

Meanwhile, Puss in Boots kept going until he came to an enormous stone castle. This castle belonged to a wicked ogre. The ogre was very rich—and the actual owner of all the fields the king's carriage had passed.

Puss in Boots knocked on the door. When the ogre's servants answered, Puss in Boots asked to be taken to see their master at once. The servants had never seen a cat wearing boots before so they led him straight to the ogre's room.

Puss in Boots bowed low. "I have come to pay my respects," he said, "for I have heard that you are a very remarkable person!"

"So I am," said the ogre.

"I have even been told," Puss in Boots went on, "that you can turn yourself into any creature in the world—even a proud lion! However, I do not believe this can possibly be true."

"Don't you?" cried the ogre, most insulted. Then to prove his powers, he turned himself into a great roaring lion.

"How remarkable," said Puss in Boots,

taking a step backward, for he was rather afraid of lions. "You truly amaze me! I have also been told that you can turn yourself into a tiny mouse. But I am sure that is quite impossible!"

"Impossible?" roared the ogre. "Just watch!" Then, quick as a wink, he turned himself into a little grey mouse and scampered across the floor.

Puss in Boots wasted no time. He quickly pounced on the tiny mouse and ate him up!

Just then the king's carriage drew up to the palace gates. Puss in Boots dusted himself off and ran outside to meet them.

30

As the king and the princess stepped
down from the carriage, Puss in Boots hailed
them, "Welcome, your majesty, to the home
of my lord and master, the Marquis of
Carabas!"

The miller's son was very surprised, but
he quickly recovered himself and showed his
guests inside.

All the servants clapped and cheered,
"Long live the Marquis of Carabas!" The
wicked ogre had treated them very badly,
and they were happy to have a new master.

The king was quite impressed with the palace and thought to himself that the Marquis of Carabas must be a wealthy, powerful man. So he offered his daughter's hand in marriage to the happy miller's son.

The beautiful princess and the Marquis of Carabas were married that day, and a splendid wedding it was!

The two of them lived together very happily for many long years.

As for Puss in Boots, his master made him a lord. And he never had to chase mice again—unless he chose to, of course!